the Brothers QUIBBLE

Aaron Blabey

PUFFIN BOOKS

For those who had sharing thrust upon them.

PUFFIN BOOKS

UK | USA | Canada | Ireland | Australia
India | New Zealand | South Africa | China

Penguin Books is part of the Penguin Random House group of companies
whose addresses can be found at global.penguinrandomhouse.com.

Penguin
Random House
Australia

First published by Penguin Group (Australia), 2014
This paperback edition published by Penguin Group (Australia), 2015

Cover and text design by Aaron Blabey and Marina Messiha © Penguin Group (Australia)
Colour separation by Splitting Image Colour Studio, Clayton, Victoria
Printed and bound in China

Cataloguing-in-Publication data is available from the National Library of Australia

ISBN 978 0 14 350706 2

puffin.com.au

Spalding Quibble ruled the roost.

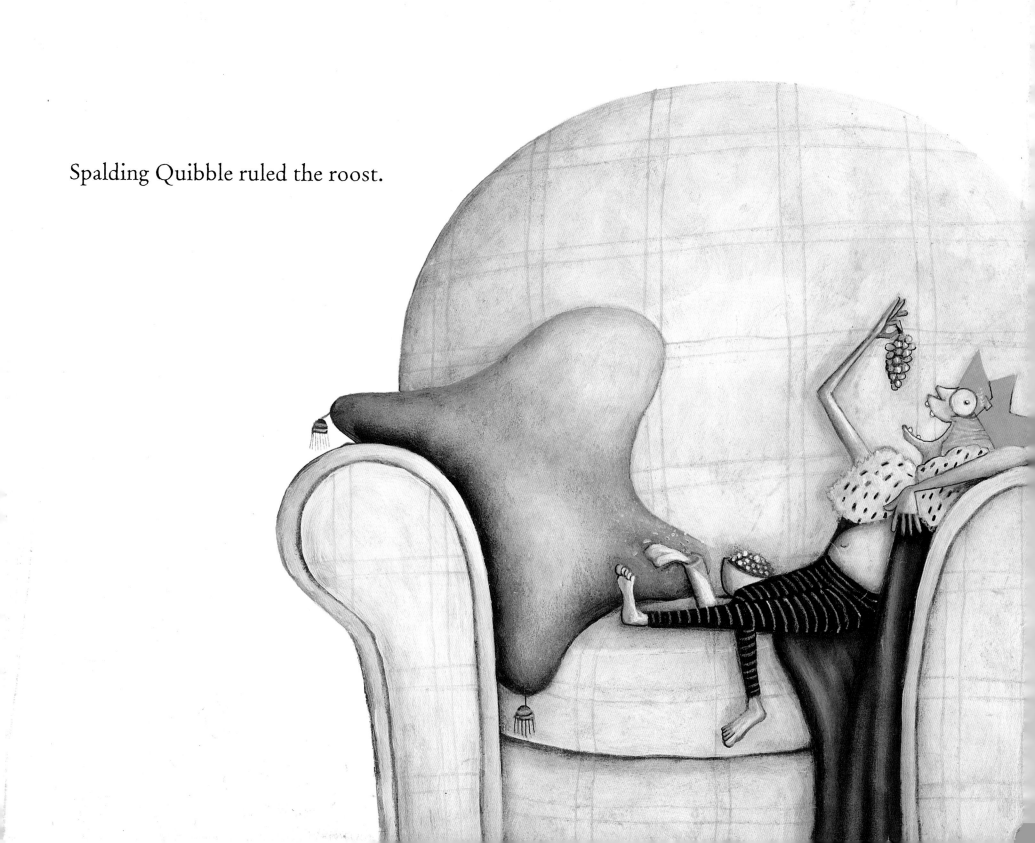

He shared it with no other.

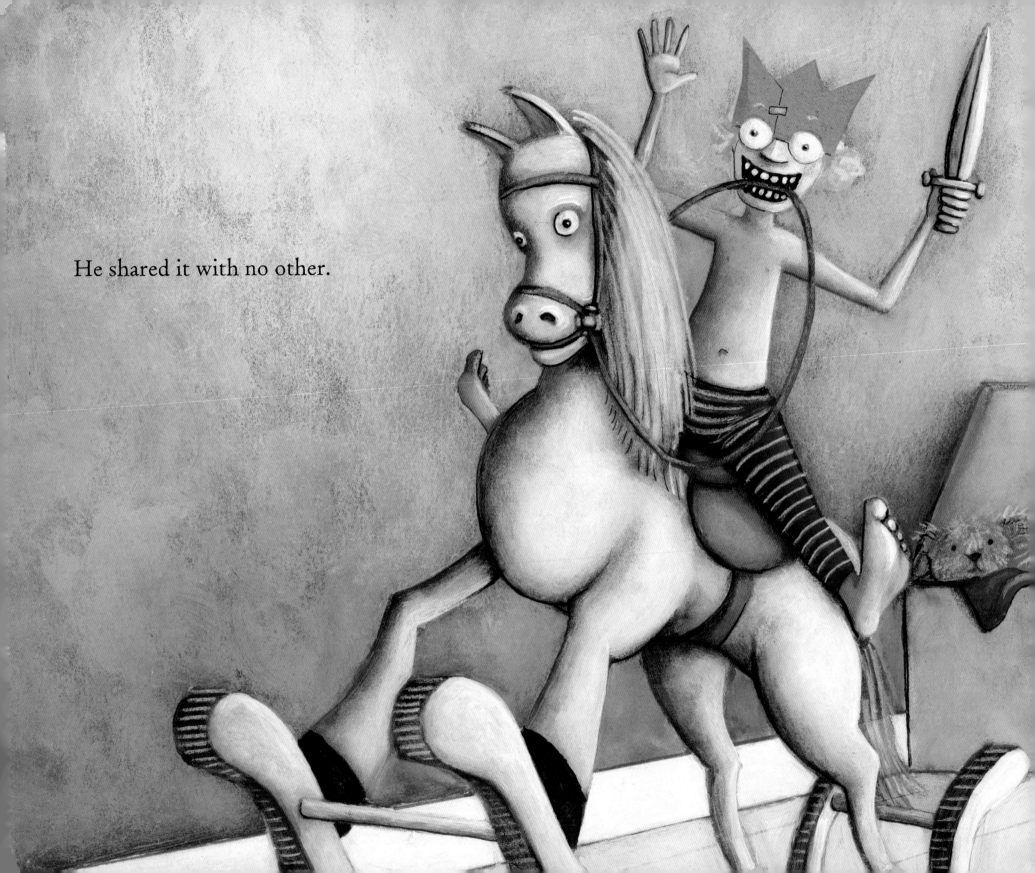

But then his parents introduced . . .

. . . a brand new baby brother.

Spalding didn't understand.
He felt a bit delirious.
He took his mother by the hand
and said, 'You can't be serious?'

'Is this some sort of joke?' he cried.
'It really isn't funny.'
'Hush now, Spalding,' mother sighed,
'And say hello to . . .

. . . Bunny.'

Mother kissed her babe to sleep.
Father watched with pride.
And Spalding felt a feeling creep
from somewhere deep inside.

IT'S A
BOY!

'Curse you, Devil!' Spalding spat

then ran and slammed the door.

'I rule the roost and that is that!
From now on this means

WAR!'

And so began young Spalding's spree
of unprovoked attacks.

He traumatised his family
and no one could relax.

His mother's nerves were shot to bits.
His father's head was balding.

And Bunny's life was just the pits.
Oh, what to do with Spalding?

For months on end they lived in gloom.
And all day long they'd shout,
'SPALDING! GO!
GET IN YOUR ROOM!
WE'VE HAD
ENOUGH...

...TIME OUT!'

But time did pass. Yes, pass it did.
And Bunny Quibble grew.
He grew into an actual kid.
Yes, that's what babies do.

He learned to sit. He learned to crawl.
He even learned to walk.
He learned to dodge a cricket ball.
And then . . .

. . . he learned to talk.

SPALDING!

And when young Bunny found his voice
and spoke that simple word –

SPALDING!
SPALDING!
SPALDING!
SPALDING!
SPALDING!
SPALDING!
SPALDING!
SPALDING!
SPALDING!
SPALDING!
SPALDING!
SPALDING!
SPALDING!
SPALDING!
SPALDING!
SPALDING!
SPALDING!
SPALDING!

Well, things did change. Oh yes! Rejoice!
A miracle occured.

You see, despite the pain that came
with every whack or shove,
Bunny spoke his brother's name
with nothing less than love.

With every word or game he'd play . . .

. . . or every cheerful scribble . . .

. . . Bunny seemed to only say,
'I love you, Spalding Quibble.'

And even when the bully boy
was sentenced to Time Out . . .

. . . Bunny would invent a ploy
to break his brother out.

In time, he slowly came to see
that living with his brother
was not a TOTAL tragedy.

In fact, they liked each other.

Of course, it wasn't always grand.

Nor was it always sunny.

And Spalding came to understand . . .

And slowly all this love began
to thaw young Spalding's heart.

His evil-minded master plan?

It gently fell apart.

But even though it comes to blows.
And EVERY DAY they fight . . .

These days, Spalding sort of knows . . .

. . . that Bunny is all right.